Snow and the Earth

Nikki Bundey

 Carolrhoda Books, Inc. / Minneapolis

First American edition published in 2001 by
Carolrhoda Books, Inc.

All the words that appear in **bold** type are explained
in the glossary that starts on page 30.

Lorna Delaney 14t, 28t; Liba Taylor 13 / Vanessa S Boeye 16t, 28b / Hutchison
Picture Library; Mike McQueen 21b / Impact Photos; John Shaw 6,
9t, 23b, 27t / Mike Lane 10 / A.N.T. 12t / Eric Soder 12b, 23t / Mirko Stelzner 16b /
Dan Griggs 19b / Hellio & Van Ingen 24t / Susanne Danegger 25b / David E Myers
26 / NHPA; Fritz Polking—cover (inset) right / Klein/Hubert—title page / Robert
Mackinlay 4 / Clyde H Smith 7 / Horst Schafer 8 / Andre Maslennikov 9b / Thomas D
Mangelsen 11t, 27b / NASA 11b / Diane Blell 18 / Alan Watson 19t / Patrick Bertrand
21t / Mark Carwardine 24b / Thierry Thomas 25t / Still Pictures; O Semenenko—
cover (background) / H Rogers—cover (inset) left, 15, / Streano/Havens 5 / J Ellard
14b / Viesti Collection 17 / W Jacobs 20 / V Larionov 22 / TRIP.

Illustrations by Artistic License/Genny Haines, Tracy Fennell

Carolrhoda Books, Inc.
A division of Lerner Publishing Group
241 First Avenue North
Minneapolis, MN 55401 U.S.A.

Website address: www.lernerbooks.com

A ZOË BOOK

Copyright © 2000 Zoë Books Limited. Originally produced in 2000 by Zoë Books
Limited, Winchester, England

Library of Congress Cataloging-in-Publication Data

Bundey, Nikki, 1948–
　　Snow and the earth / by Nikki Bundey
　　　p. cm. — (The science of weather)
　　Includes index.
　　Summary: Discusses how snow is formed in the atmosphere, the various forms
it takes when falling to earth, the conditions snow creates on the earth, and its effect
on plants and animals.
　　ISBN 1-57505-471-X (lib. bdg. : alk. paper)
　　1. Snow—Juvenile literature. [1. Snow.] I. Title. II. Series: Bundey, Nikki,
1948– The science of weather.
QC926.37.B85　　　2001
551.57′84—dc21　　　　　　　　　　　　　　　00-027919

Printed in Italy by Grafedit SpA
Bound in the United States of America
1 2 3 4 5 6—OS—06 05 04 03 02 01

CONTENTS

WILL WE HAVE SNOW?

The weather is cold, and the clouds are dark. This is a day for snow. What is snow like? Cold and white...crisp and crunchy...wet and slushy...dry and powdery? What is snow?

Snow is a form of frozen water. Water is a **liquid** that can freeze into a **solid** called ice. Its **freezing point** is 32 degrees Fahrenheit. Above that **temperature**, ice melts into water.

Clouds are factories for rain and snow. Snow never falls when the skies are clear and blue, no matter how cold it is.

In very cold weather, water droplets freeze into solid **crystals**. We call these crystals **snowflakes**. The snowflakes float down to the earth's surface.

The layer of invisible **gases** around the earth is called the **atmosphere**. These gases make up the air we breathe. One of the gases is **water vapor**. As water vapor cools, tiny **water droplets** form around specks of dust. The droplets make up the clouds we see in the sky.

In cold weather, the droplets freeze into crystals. They grow big and heavy and fall as snow. In warm weather, droplets become rain.

See for Yourself

Ask an adult to help you.
- Press snow in your hands to make a snowball.
- Put the snowball in a saucepan on a stove.
- Heat the snowball until it starts to bubble and steam.
- Your snow has passed through three states. What are they?

AGAIN AND AGAIN

The earth's water supplies are renewed all the time. This process is called the **water cycle**. Rain and snow are part of the cycle. Another name for rain and snow is **precipitation**.

The water cycle begins when rain or snow falls. Some of it falls into the oceans and some on land. Rain and snow that fall on land drain into streams and rivers, which then flow into lakes and oceans.

Snowfall is one stage in the water cycle, which keeps the world green and fresh. About two-thirds of our planet is covered in water.

Melting snow feeds mountain streams. The streams rush down steep slopes and tumble over waterfalls. They join up with larger rivers, which flow through valleys and plains to the sea.

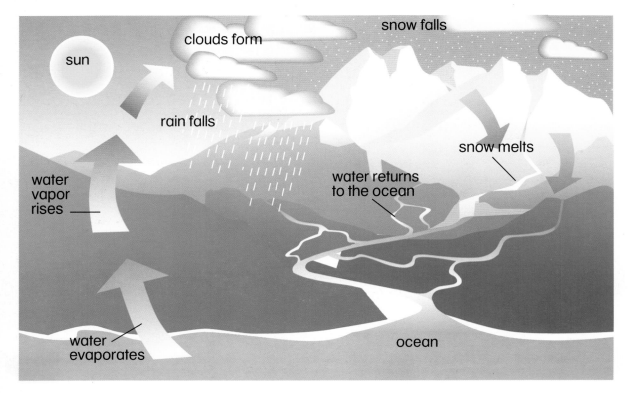

clouds form

snow falls

sun

rain falls

snow melts

water vapor rises

water returns to the ocean

water evaporates

ocean

Snow that falls on the ocean usually melts at once. Seawater is salty and has a lower freezing point than freshwater. The sea freezes only in very cold places.

The sun heats the surface of the earth and the oceans. The sun's heat turns some water from the liquid state into water vapor. This process is called **evaporation**. Hot gases rise. The water vapor rises with the warm air.

High in the atmosphere, the air becomes very cold. The water vapor cools and turns into droplets, forming clouds. This process is called **condensation**. As the droplets grow larger, they turn into rain or snow.

SNOWFLAKE MAGIC

Snowflakes are made up of many tiny ice crystals that freeze together. The biggest snowflakes may measure up to 2.5 inches from side to side. They contain hundreds of ice crystals.

Each snowflake is very beautiful, and each one is completely different from the next. However, all snowflakes are **hexagonal**, or six-sided. They may look like rods, needles, plates, or feathery stars.

This type of cloud is called **nimbostratus**. It forms a dark, low blanket and often brings precipitation. Snowflakes or rain may fall, depending on small changes in air temperature.

You can best see the fantastic structure of a snowflake through a **microscope**. These snowflakes look like six-pointed stars.

Why do snowflakes form in the ways they do? It may look like magic, but the answer lies in science. The shapes and sizes of the crystals are caused by weather conditions. How high and how cold is the cloud where the crystals are forming? How much water does the cloud hold? Star- and needle-shaped crystals form in moist conditions. Plate-shaped crystals form when the air is drier.

Snowflakes come in all kinds of shapes. Scientists call them needles, plates, cups, and columns. A snowflake that looks like a tree is called a **dendrite**.

SNOWSTORMS

The heaviest snowfalls occur when the air temperature is around the freezing point. The snowflakes are pulled down to earth by the force of **gravity**. The bigger the snowflakes, the more the air slows them down as they fall. Smaller snowflakes slip through the air more quickly. Falling snow may be heavy and wet or dry and crisp.

When the air is still, snowflakes float gently down to earth. They often stick together as they fall.

A blizzard hits the state of Alaska. Very strong winds blow during blizzards. Temperatures are often very low, and the snow is powdery. Blizzards strike with the greatest force in wide-open places, such as mountainsides.

Air currents, or winds, may catch hold of the snowflakes. The wind whirls the flakes around. High winds can whip a heavy snowfall into a **blizzard**. In a strong wind, the snow falls at a slant, or angle. It can be very hard to see during a blizzard. Sometimes blizzards create a total **whiteout**.

During a whiteout, it is very hard to see where the land ends and the sky begins. People can easily get lost. Whiteout conditions are common in Antarctica.

11

ICY SHOWERS

Sometimes we see towering, puffy clouds. These are called **cumulonimbus clouds**. These clouds often form on hot summer days. Inside these clouds, icy balls of **hail** may form.

Most hailstones are about the size of a pea, but some can weigh as much as 26 ounces and can break windows.

The temperature inside the clouds can change quickly, causing air to rush up and down. Ice crystals inside the clouds are tossed up and down, too. As the crystals melt and freeze again, new layers of ice form. The crystals become hailstones, which are smooth balls of ice. They are much harder and heavier than snowflakes.

Hailstones fall quickly through the sky. They strike the ground with such force that they often bounce up again.

Rain that is partly frozen is called sleet. It falls with a wet splash. If the temperature rises, sleet turns into rain. If the temperature drops, sleet can become snow.

Depending on temperature and air conditions within a cloud, precipitation can take other forms. Small grains of falling ice are called snow pellets. These are harder and rounder than snowflakes but softer than hailstones. Other kinds of precipitation are **sleet** and freezing rain.

ON THE GROUND

Some snowflakes melt as soon as they land on the ground. Some stick to other flakes to form a thick layer. Fallen snow may be deep and powdery or wet and slushy. If snow melts slightly during the day and then refreezes as night falls, it will form a hard, crunchy crust.

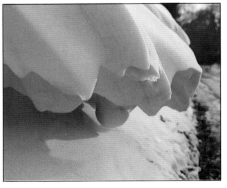

The wind can blow the snow into beautiful shapes.

The wind may blow loose snow into high banks called drifts. Snow that lies on the ground for a long time may become packed solid and hard.

During the day, the snow on this roof begins to melt in the warm sunshine. Later, the drops freeze to form icicles.

See for Yourself

As snow melts and freezes, it takes up different amounts of space.

- Fill a dish with loose snow and measure the depth.

- Let the snow melt. How deep is the water?

- Leave the dish in the freezer.

- Measure the depth of the ice.

When snow begins to thaw, snowdrifts may turn into puddles. The melting snow mixes with soil and makes fields and paths muddy.

Deep, packed snow may form layers that slip and slide. Huge gaps and cracks, called **crevasses**, may open up.

As the temperature rises, the snow turns to slush and then **meltwater**. This water may sink into the soil, evaporate, or drain into lakes, streams, and rivers. Melting snows can cause floods.

SNOWY CLIMATES

The typical weather in a region over a long period is called **climate**. The weather changes with the **seasons**. The earth tilts at an angle as it circles the sun. The places on earth leaning away from the sun have winter cold, while those places leaning toward the sun enjoy summer warmth.

The **polar regions** of the Arctic and Antarctic have a bitterly cold climate with snow and ice all year. Wide plains called **tundra** surround the Arctic regions. In the tundra, snow melts for only a short time in summer.

We often think of deserts as very hot places, but many deserts can be very cold. The Gobi Desert in northeastern Asia often has snow during the winter.

When snow melts on the surface of the tundra, large pools of water form. The water cannot sink into the soil because it is still frozen below the surface. The pools freeze up again in autumn.

Temperate regions of North America and Europe receive snowstorms in winter, between December and April.

Great belts of forests are found south of the Arctic tundra in Canada, Scandinavia, and Russia. These regions have very heavy winter snowfalls, but their summers are generally warm. Lands with milder climates are called **temperate**. In temperate regions, snow is less common, except in winter.

SNOW ON MOUNTAINS

The higher you go up a mountain, the colder the air gets. The types of plants growing on the mountainside change with the height. Toward the top, there may be no plants at all, just bare rock and ice. Snowstorms are common on the slopes of high mountains. The peaks may be capped with snow all year round.

Mount Kilimanjaro towers over the hot plains of East Africa, south of the **equator**. The mountain's main peak rises to more than 19,500 feet above sea level. The peak is always capped with snow.

Winds from the Pacific Ocean carry water vapor to Mount Rainier in the state of Washington. Huge amounts of snow fall on its slopes. In just twelve months in 1971 and 1972, the snowfall measured more than 93 feet. This was a world record.

Many mountains play a part in making snow. Winds sweep in from the ocean, carrying moisture. When they meet a steep mountain range, they are forced upward and cool rapidly. They can drop large amounts of rain or snow on the **windward** slopes of the mountain.

Sometimes a wall of snow tumbles down a mountainside. This event is called an **avalanche**. A rise in temperature or an earthquake may loosen the snow, or a new fall of heavy snow may cause the snow beneath to give way.

RIVERS OF SNOW AND ICE

The snow on mountaintops builds up over many years. Fresh falls of snow press down on the snow underneath. The weight turns the bottom layers into solid ice.

The ice begins to move, forming **glaciers**. They are rivers of ice that move very slowly down the mountainside. The ice carries along boulders and stones. Moving ice can carve a valley through solid rock. Some glaciers reach the coast. The ends of the glaciers break into chunks that float out to sea as **icebergs**.

The weight of a glacier makes it slide downhill. It is pulled down by the force of gravity. The weight of the glacier melts the ice just enough to allow the glacier to move forward. This glacier is in New Zealand.

Many thousands of years ago, glaciers made these deep inlets in the coast of Norway. They are called **fjords**.

Melting snow can form powerful rivers. River water carves out valleys and narrow **ravines** from rock. **Erosion** is the process in which water, ice, rain, snow, and wind wear away and shape a landscape.

Melting snows from high in the Himalaya Mountains feed the great Ganges River. The water flows more than 1,550 miles to the sea.

,NOW AND PLANTS

Snow is cold, but it can act like a warm blanket on the ground. It protects young plants from cold winds and sharp **frosts**.

Snow can damage plants, too. It may press down on them, snapping stems and twigs. Fir trees can stand up to heavy snow because their branches are tough and springy.

Many spruce trees grow in this snowy forest in Russia. Their tough needles can survive in very hard winters.

The highest mountain range in western Europe is the Alps. The edelweiss plant grows there. Edelweiss protects itself from winter blizzards by growing low to the ground.

Plants that grow on snowy mountains are called **alpines**. Most alpines hug the ground. Their small stems and leaves are hard to break. Many alpines grow in sheltered cracks and crevices in the rock.

All plants need water to grow, and melting snow gives them plenty of it. During the summer months, high mountain pastures and even the Arctic tundra burst into flower.

A blanket of snow protects tundra plants during the Arctic winter. They flower again in summer. There are mosses, lichens, and wildflowers such as purple saxifrage. Animals, from tiny insects to huge caribou, depend on the plants for survival.

SNOWBIRDS

In polar regions and other cold places, the ground is frozen and covered with snow for most of the year. It is hard for birds to find plants and insects to eat in cold places.

Many birds have adapted to snowy conditions. The snowy owl of the Arctic has white feathers that act as **camouflage** against the snow. The feathers help the owls get close to their **prey** without being seen. The feathers also hide the owls from hunters.

Most owls hunt at night and nest in trees. The snowy owl is different. This owl nests on the ground because there are not many trees in the Arctic. It cannot hunt under cover of darkness because the Arctic is light both day and night in summer.

The ptarmigan changes color with the seasons. In summer it is brown and black, like the tundra, but in winter it is snow white.

Emperor penguins breed on the icy coasts of Antarctica. They huddle together for shelter against the blizzards. While the female penguins are away fishing at sea, the males look after the baby penguins.

In temperate climates, many hungry birds visit backyard bird feeders during snowy winters.

The seasonal patterns of thawing and freezing affect the lives of many birds. In summer, the Arctic has plenty of food, so birds **migrate** northward. They breed in the Arctic and return south with the first snows of winter.

See for Yourself

After a fresh fall of snow, you will probably see the tracks of birds and animals in the snow.
- Copy the shapes into a notebook.
- Measure them with a ruler.
- Try to identify which birds made which tracks. Check a bird book in your local library for help.

ANIMALS IN THE SNOW

Reptiles are **cold-blooded**. They cannot survive without warm sunshine. Birds and **mammals** have built-in central heating systems. They are **warm-blooded** creatures, so they can survive in snowy and icy conditions. Arctic mammals, such as polar bears, foxes, and hares, have furry or hairy coats. They stay warm even in the coldest blizzards.

The polar bear lives in the Arctic. Its white fur helps it hide against the snow. The soles of the bear's feet are hairy. They help the bear grip slippery ice and snow.

A caribou searches for plants to eat on the snowy ground in Alaska.

Like birds, some mammals change colors with the seasons. Northern hares and ermines have white fur in winter for camouflage in the snow. Reindeer and caribou use their hooves to scrape away snow from the mosses and lichens that they eat. Their hooves are broad, so that the animals do not slip and sink in slush and mud during the thaw.

As the days grow shorter and the temperature drops, ermines of the far north turn from brown to white, in time for the winter snows. Only the tip of the tail remains black.

LIFE AND DEATH

Snow brings fun for young people, while older people may see it as a nuisance. We sometimes forget that snow, like rain, fills our planet with freshwater. Clean freshwater keeps humans, animals, and plants alive.

When snow is on the ground it often becomes dirty. It can even be **polluted** while still in the air. Water vapor may mix with exhaust fumes from cars and smoke from factories. The polluted water vapor may then turn into **acid snow**.

Melting snow provides us with water for drinking, for watering crops, and for giving to animals.

In Mongolia, a country in central Asia, smoke from fires and factories pollutes the air and the snow.

Pollution in the air may be warming up the temperature of our planet. This change, called **global warming**, is already affecting life in the Arctic and Antarctic. Warmer conditions have changed the life cycles of fish and other prey eaten by polar bears. Many bears are already starving. We must look after our planet and keep it as fresh as the purest snow.

See for Yourself

- Fill a saucepan with snow and let it melt.

- Pour the water through a paper coffee filter.

- How many specks of dust and dirt are left behind?

GLOSSARY

acid snow	Snow that has been polluted by chemicals in the air
air current	A movement of air, also called wind
alpine	Any plant that grows on high mountains
atmosphere	The layer of gases around a planet
avalanche	A massive fall of snow down a mountainside
blizzard	A heavy snowstorm with high winds
camouflage	Coloring or markings that help animals blend with their surroundings
climate	The typical weather in one place over a long period
cold-blooded	Unable to keep warm without the sun's heat
condensation	Turning from a gas into a liquid
crevasse	A crack in deep snow or ice
crystal	A substance, such as ice, arranged into a geometric pattern
cumulonimbus cloud	A towering, billowing thunder cloud
dendrite	A snowflake with a branching shape, like a tree
equator	An imaginary line around the middle of the earth
erosion	The wearing down of rock by wind, rain, frost, or water
evaporation	The change from liquid into gas
fjord	A deep sea inlet, made by a moving glacier
freezing point	The temperature at which water turns to ice (32°F)
frost	A covering of ice crystals
gas	An airy substance that fills any space in which it is contained
glacier	A river of ice fed by compressed snow from a mountaintop
global warming	The warming of the earth, possibly caused by air pollution
gravity	The force that pulls objects to earth
hail	Hard balls of ice that fall during thunderstorms
hexagonal	Six-sided
iceberg	A large slab of ice that floats through the sea
liquid	A fluid substance, such as water
mammal	A warm-blooded animal that feeds on its mother's milk
meltwater	Water left behind after snow has melted

microscope	An instrument that makes tiny objects look larger
migrate	To travel at regular seasons in search of food or breeding grounds
nimbostratus cloud	A low cloud that blankets the sky and often produces snow
polar regions	Areas around the earth's most northerly and southerly points
polluted	Poisoned or made impure
precipitation	Any kind of rain, snow, or hail
prey	An animal that is hunted
ravine	A deep, narrow valley carved by water
reptiles	A group of cold-blooded animals including snakes, crocodiles, and tortoises
seasons	Winter, spring, summer, and fall, caused by the tilting of the earth
sleet	Frozen or partly frozen rain
snowflake	A group of ice crystals that freeze together and fall to the ground
solid	A substance that has a specific form and shape, unlike a liquid or a gas
temperate	Having a mild or moderate climate
temperature	Warmth or coldness, measured in degrees
tundra	Treeless plains found in Arctic regions
warm-blooded	Having a constant, warm body temperature, regardless of the temperature of the air
water cycle	The ongoing process in which rain falls, evaporates, rises, and condenses
water droplet	A tiny drop of water. Many droplets make a raindrop, snowflake, or hailstone
water vapor	A gas created when water evaporates
whiteout	Weather conditions that fill the air with snow and make seeing difficult
windward	Facing the wind

INDEX